THE GRACIE EDMOND STORY

DIANE METTS

Copyright © 2021 by Diane Metts

All rights reserved.

No part of this book may be reproduced in any form or by any electronic or mechanical means, including information storage and retrieval systems, without written permission from the author, except for the use of brief quotations in a book review.

CONTENTS

Chapter 1	1
Chapter 2	11
Chapter 3	21
Chapter 4	31
Chapter 5	37
Chapter 6	41
Chapter 7	47
Chapter 8	53
Chapter 9	63
Chapter 10	67
Chapter 11	73

CHAPTER ONE

I STOOD outside the abortion clinic twiddling my thumbs and pacing back and forth for over an hour. I exhausted all ideas on how to get this procedure without my parents and brother getting into trouble. If I walked in there shaking like a leaf, the nurses would be onto me and call family services immediately. There was no way they would allow a fourteen-year-old to abort a baby without consent. This was all my fault. I should have run away a long time ago.

Who was going to believe me now? My family would turn against me for sure and the truth would tarnish my father's reputation as a Pastor in the community. He was admired, respected, known, and protected. Nobody would ever believe that the man who held weekly sermons and worship services was an incestophile. His belief in inbreeding was instilled from birth and was to never be discussed outside the home. The man that created me was the reason my brother felt comfortable raping me. It was considered a lifestyle, even if it meant children being born with disabilities. In his eyes, it was nothing more than harmless genetic attraction. I'd spent years envisioning ways to get me and Nettie far away from that sick household. My only other option was going to the next town over where there was an all-girls catholic orphanage I read about online at the library. They took in kids ages four through eighteen and provided meals, clothing, and shelter. All Nettie and I wanted was a fresh start, with no more sexual and physical abuse. Tears welled up in my eyes as I rubbed my tiny belly, feeling defeated once again. A sense of impending doom was settling into my stomach, making me feel nauseous. My hands began trembling, and a tightness crept into my chest. The conflicting thoughts mixed with the hot sun beaming on my head were causing a panic attack to surface. If momma found out I was at the clinic, she'd put a cattle rod to my ass for sure. Before anyone noticed, I put my hood on and shamefully walked back to the bus stop, crushed that I was a coward and had let fear win again.

When I got home Nettie was in her electric wheelchair watching tv. I wondered if my unborn baby was going to have special needs like her. From what I read, there could be congenital physical malformations or severe intellectual deficits due to this being my brother's child. I was being forced to follow through with a high-risk pregnancy like my first cousin Suzette had to. She used to sleep over every weekend as a kid, but when my brother did to her what he did to me, Nettie was conceived. At eleven years old Suzette's parents disowned her because she wouldn't tell them who the baby's father was. She was embarrassed and scared to admit her own cousin, which was her mother's nephew, had been crawling in the room at night, raping her. The days she slept over were the only nights he didn't touch me. At this time I was just a helpless five-year-old, scared of my big brother. When Suzette was four months pregnant, she was shipped back to Africa where her grandmother lived because her parents were adamant about "not raising a hoe". They made all types of accusations, called her despicable names, and tortured her until she finally took off for her flight. Her experience solidified the fact that nobody would ever believe me. My mother offered to adopt Nettie because deep down she knew the truth. She couldn't have any more kids, so she was ecstatic about having a newborn around. Two days after the birth of the baby, she flew to Africa and took Suzette's baby right from the hospital. Since it was so corrupt there, all she had to do was pay the government under the table to pass this off as a legitimate adoption instead of a kidnapping. The police went into the hospital and gave the nurses some money and made them forge a few papers and signatures. Before the ink dried, the officers took the baby out of the nursery while Suzette was sleeping. At this time my older brother was serving five years in Juvie for beating a kid in the head with brass knuckles, causing permanent brain damage. When he got out at nineteen, my life turned upside down. I was forced to live with two grown men sexually assaulting me while my mother drank herself into a drunken rage. The guilt she carried around every day made her lash out at me as if I caused all the family problems.

My brother hadn't seen me in years, so when he finally did, his eyes remained on my cleavage the whole time. It started with him caressing my legs and commenting on how big my breast had grown. I was very uncomfortable, but my father was always preaching about keeping the bloodline pure, so that's all he knew. It really wasn't his fault, it was learned behavior.

One day I asked my older brother why he wouldn't stop touching me and he simply said, "Because I am attracted to you, Gracie."

Each day that passed my anxiety got worse and so did the thoughts of killing myself. Over and over the voices in my head taunted me to commit suicide because this was not the life I wanted to live. I was a minor, so I had to go along with anything my parents believed in just to keep the peace. When Suzette got pregnant my dad tried covering it up and said nothing was wrong with incest. He had my brother's back and never faulted him once. My father preached every day about never letting outsiders into the family unit.

I never imagined things getting this bad until two months ago when my parents went away for a week and he raped me every day they were gone. I'll never forget his hot breath, rough callused hands, yellow-tinged eyes, creepy smirk, and awful body odor. One night while he was on top of me panting like a dog he whispered, "Daddy used to do it to me, now it's your turn". I knew if I told them they wouldn't care, they'd just sweep it under a rug that was already lumpy from all the lies underneath.

I tied my hair up and buried my face into my palms. My brother wasn't home yet, but any minute he would be coming through the front door. The thought of having his baby stimulated something inside of me, causing an instant gush of projectile vomit. I grabbed the White Pages off the shelf and searched for the number of the orphanage.

"Please don't come in here, please!" I pleaded in my head as I heard the doorknob jiggle, causing me to slide the white pages under the dresser. My mother had been drinking her dark liquor since early this morning and had been downstairs in a coma. Alcohol made her violent, scary, and unrecognizable. My body began shaking as I sat in the dark corner on my knees, awaiting the torture that was about to come my way.

"Come here, you dumb fuck!" she screamed as the bedroom door swung open.

I jumped to my feet and tensed up, ready for the blow.

"Didn't I ask you to wash the dishes?" She smirked, standing over me with one hand on her hip and the other balled into a fist.

Her short, stiff brown hair was no longer resting neatly on her shoulders, but sticking up in every

direction. In the dark, her yellow eyes looked as if they were glowing like a hyena hiding in a cave.

"And what's this?" she asked, pulling a granola bar wrapper from under my bed.

"I thought I told you no food until this house is cleaned from top to bottom, you lazy little bitch. You think because you're able to conceive and I can't that you're better than me?" she yelled, yanking me by my thin ponytail.

"You're just like your cousin, Suzie. Stupid and worthless. We should have taken your monkey ass to the sex trafficking auction and made some money when we had the chance," she hissed.

She dragged my small-framed, sore, fragile body all the way to the kitchen sink. Nettie was sitting in her wheelchair finishing the rest of her liquid feeding from a straw. The dishes were stacked high, still covered in leftover food from yesterday. When my awful mother walked away to watch

her afternoon soap opera, I picked up as many food morsels my quivering fingers would allow and scarfed what I could down my throat. I hadn't had a meal since yesterday morning because she said I was a brat that needed to learn how to listen and follow directions. Lately, I had been assaulting my father when they try to rape me. Whenever I leave a mark, they take it out on my mother. That was when these drunk outbursts occurred, causing her to resent me more and more each day.

When she told me to do the dishes earlier, I forgot because I had become so consumed with writing down my escape plan and cleaning after the family dog. Since Nettie was handicapped, I was responsible for the upkeep of the house. My mother insisted she was too depressed and my father was too busy trying to convince the community he was family man of the year. The dog ate and got treated better than I ever had in my entire existence on this Earth.

My head continued to throb as I finished the last

few dishes. Every time she pulled me by my ponytail, a migraine would surface, causing me to vomit and lie in the dark for hours. The last thing I wanted was to throw up the only scrapes I was able to get my hands on. Interrupting my thoughts, my mother walked in, scanning the kitchen, making sure it was up to par.

"Looks good, now sweep the floor and scram," she announced, wheeling my sister in front of the television. She took her plate off the coffee table and tossed three small pieces of breakfast sausage into the dog's bowl. My eyes got big, and a subtle smile spread across my face. I did my last few duties and looked around to make sure the coast was clear.

When I didn't hear a peep, I got on all fours and ate the sausage intended for Sandy, our terrier. It didn't bother me that small pieces of wet dog food were mixed in because over time I was able to block out the taste. Just as I was finishing and ready to stand, I felt a hard, swift kick to the back of my head.

"So now you're a thief, huh? You rather steal

Sandy's food than wait until I grant you permission to eat, you ugly cunt?" she asked, standing over me. Before I could get a word out, she snatched me by my left ear and back into the dark bedroom I had been in all day. Before I knew it, the back of her hand was coming toward my face. I braced myself for the sting and prayed to God, who I was beginning to think didn't exist because why would he make me suffer when I'd done nothing wrong. Due to the increasing pressure in my skull, I dropped to my knees and became one with the floorboards. Before walking away, she pulled a half-smoked cigarette from the back of her ear, lit it, and took a huge drag.

" I tried to be nice, but you wanna steal food and be sneaky. Not only did u take the dog's food, but you hid evidence under the bed yesterday." She exhaled, blowing the smoke in my face.

"I tried to be the perfect mother and wife but noooooooooo people wanna test me," she

complained, leaning against the door. I curled up in a ball, refusing to give her the eye contact she wanted. I hated myself for being born and wanted so badly to end this thing called life. Tears fell from my eyes onto the dusty wood. Every part of my body was stinging and throbbing from the physical and sexual abuse over the years. I heard her approaching and once again tensed up.

"Ahhhhhh," I cried as she put out her cigarette on my shoulder blade.

"Now stay in here until I give you permission to leave, you dirty little thief. Don't let your father and brother come to me saying you won't give'em no cutty either, or you're really going to wish I took you to that auction," she muttered, exiting the room, making sure to slam the door. I sat up and wiped the tears from my face. As I always did, I looked out the nailed shut window and contemplated more ideas on my escape.

CHAPTER TWO

"Nettie, wake up. Now's our chance to get out of here," I said, shaking her out of her sleep.

She had a speech delay, so she was nonverbal, but I knew she understood what I was saying. Her eyes got big, and she pointed to the closet, indicating for me to get her coat.

"Good, Nettie, now you can't make any noises or Carl will wake up, understand?"

She shook her head yes and allowed me to put her socks and shoes on. I looked at the clock and it was ten minutes before midnight. Everyone in the house went to bed around ten, so I was hoping they were in a deep sleep by now.

Once my sister was ready, I picked her fragile fifty-pound body up and placed her in her electric wheelchair. The last bus would be coming in five minutes, and I didn't want to miss it.

Before leaving, I went into my room and grabbed some last minute necessities I might need at the orphanage.

Hairbrush, hygiene products, fifty dollars in cash, and my cellphone were all I packed.

"Nettie, you ready?" I asked, tip-toeing into her room.

Bam!

I was now on the floor, holding the back of my head in pain. My brother, Carl, punched me so hard I was seeing double.

"Where were you taking my precious Nettie?!" Carl asked, standing over me with a balled up trembling fist.

"Just for a walk, she couldn't sleep," I lied.

"A walk at midnight, huh? Do I look like I was born yesterday? I been in your shoes before. When I was a young boy, I wanted to run away but eventually, you get used to being touched. Dad played with my private parts and made me suck his when I was a kid, even when it made me uncomfortable. You'll both have to endure the same pain until you realize there is no way out," he confessed.

"Please, just let me go back to my room," I pleaded.

He backed up, smirked, and grabbed Nettie out of her wheelchair, and placed her back in bed, never removing his eyes off me.

"Let's go," he demanded, yanking me off the ground by my hair.

I wanted to scream so badly, but the thought of my parents shutting the door and putting in earplugs was too much to bear again.

"Carl, stop, please!" I cried as he ripped off my shirt.

"Gracie wants to learn the hard way, so I'm going to show you who's boss," he taunted while pulling my pants down to my ankles.

I began punching him repeatedly in the face and chest, but with all the muscle he gained in juvie, it was no use. When I wouldn't stop swinging, he took his belt off and wrapped it around my wrist, then secured it to the metal bed frame. Next, he pulled my panties down and rammed his ashy, curved penis into my already swollen vagina.

"Why would you do this to me when I'm pregnant?" I whimpered in disgust.

"Pregnant or not ima teach you a lesson you'll never forget," he huffed while continuing his aggressive offbeat stroke.

Tears rolled out the corner of my eyes onto the white bedsheets. I was never going to get Nettie and me out of this house alive. My plan B was to go alone and come back for her with the police.

"Ahhhhhh, yessssss! mhm!" Carl moaned in pleasure.

He pulled his dick out, allowing the remaining cum to fall onto my thigh. The piece of paper with the address and number of the orphanage fell out of my pocket when he took off my pants. He picked it up, read it, then ripped it into a million pieces before tossing it into my face.

"Now go to bed!" he yelled, releasing the belt and walking out.

When the door flew open for the first time in two days, I shielded my face, preparing to be hit by Carl once again. The escape stunt I pulled the other day made me lose all privileges, including food. If wanted to make it out, I'd have to cooperate the best I could.

"Let's go wash up," Carl stated, standing over me with three towels on his shoulder.

"I don't want a shower," I lied, sitting in my urine and feces.

"Kids don't make choices in this house. Now get off the floor and let's go, the water is running!" he demanded, pinching his nose in disgust.

Scared he would take his belt off again, I followed his command. As I stood up, I became dizzy and felt the baby move for the very first time in days. The sensation made my heart sink because I was hoping I miscarried. No child deserved to be brought into a sick family like this.

When I walked into the bathroom, my father was already in the shower.

"Hop in," my brother ordered.

If I wanted to execute my second plan, I'd have to obey him for now, so I did what I was told.

I stepped in and gagged at the grin on my father's face.

"Nettie is sick with a cold so I can't play with her for a while," he informed, moving a strand of hair out of my face and behind my ear.

"Carl said you tried to take our precious sex toy and we can't have that happen again, you hear?"

He took my shaking hand and rubbed it against his wet, prickly chest. We were now standing face to face as my brother dropped his clothes, preparing to join.

I closed my eyes and clenched my teeth the moment my father began sucking my nipples. It saddened me that my first sexual experience was with my immediate family members.

"I'll handle her from the back, pops," my brother announced, stepping in and instantly spreading my ass cheeks apart with excessive force.

My only option right now was to suck it up and cry later. One thing I came to realize over the years was that crying never changed anything.

"Suck it," my dad barked.

He had a punch that could knock out a horse, so I obeyed without further hesitation.

As soon as I bent over, Carl rammed his penis into my vagina, causing me to lose balance.

"Nettie is handicapped and she can do a better blow job than that. Put some effort into it if you want to eat tonight," my father said.

I swished his penis back and forth in my mouth, trying to block out the salty taste. Despite being covered with water, I could still taste the sodium and feel the grit on my tongue as if I had eaten a dirty clam. It was easier to ignore Carl's strokes because his dick was only semi-hard and shriveled up like a raisin.

"Yeaaaaa, there we go, that a girl!" they both chanted.

My father's eyes rolled into the back of his head, indicating the release of semen was near. After today, I was going to befriend Carl just enough for him to allow me outside again. This time everything will be packed, and Nettie would have to stay until I came back with help.

"Take those strokes like a woman. No man will ever fuck you like me," Carl recited.

"Ahhhhhh! Yes! Oh, my god! It's coming!"

Before I knew it, warm, slimy cum hit the back of my throat. I spit it on his foot, causing his reflexes to knee me in the jaw and on to the hard ceramic tub.

I curled into a fetal position, hoping he wouldn't strike again. Blood oozed from my nose into the water, then down the drain.

"I'll finish with you tomorrow," Carl stated, stepping out of the shower with my father. He threw a towel and white t-shirt at me and said, "Get dressed and return to your room."

Another two days had passed, and Carl was starting to come around. He allowed me to have water and a few pieces of bread with butter. My time was spent reciting the address to the orphanage and imagining a life with parents that loved me. After all I had experienced over the years, nothing was going to stop me from getting on that bus in the morning.

Abruptly, the door flew open, causing me to lose my train of thought.

"I need you to watch Nettie tomorrow since I got to take mom and dad to their appointments. I'm trusting that you learned your lesson," Carl declared.

"I did, and I'm sorry that I ever tried to leave. You've done so much for me, and I ought to be a little more grateful. Your my world, having your baby is an honor," I lied.

Carl smiled and walked toward me with open arms. The thought of him touching my body made me want to jump out of my skin. I inhaled deeply and forced a fake smile. He hugged me tight, lifting my feet off the floor as my arms remained stiffly by my side.

"I knew you'd come around sooner or later. It gets better, I promise. Like I said, I've been in your shoes before but eventually, you get used to the incest way of life. Why should we share our bloodline with strangers? I want to be your first, just like dad was my first," he confessed trying to convince me.

"Yeah, Nettie needs another sibling to keep her company for sure. From now on, you won't have to worry about me being defiant. I'm starting to understand you and Dad's p-point of v-view after all," I stuttered.

"That's my girl," Carl commented, pinching my cheek before walking out.

The minute he pulled out the driveway in the morning I was making a run for it. I felt bad about leaving Nettie, but this is what's best for both of us.

Due to my compliance, Carl invited me to join the family at the dinner table that night. I didn't think I would ever get over the feeling of having to sit amongst my abuser and pass bread like nothing was wrong. My mother never came to check on me the whole four days I was locked in that room. I could have been dead in there and she wouldn't have known. Even when I sat across from her, she never looked up and acknowledged my busted lip or five-pound weight loss. She had many demons and felt guilty that she couldn't give my father more kids when he wanted a big family. It was a tradition where we were from and made her feel less of a woman. The doctor said she was lucky to have two and that having another could be fatal due to her severe endometriosis. They made her get a hysterectomy, which was what started the downward spiral into depression. Her main reason for adopting Nettie was so my dad could turn her into a baby factory as soon as her period came. I belonged to Carl, and Nettie belonged to him.

CHAPTER THREE

Since getting off lockdown, I was now able to do my normal routine, which was getting Nettie ready in the morning. I washed her down, helped her into the wheelchair, then fed her oatmeal with bananas. Carl would be leaving in two hours since my parent's appointment was at nine in the morning. They were an old school African couple that never got their driver's license when coming to this country, so my brother had to drive them everywhere.

"I'm coming back to rescue you. I promise," I whispered in Nettie's ear.

I could tell she wanted to say something so bad, but her brain wouldn't allow it. A single tear rolled down her soft brown cheek, and it was moments like this I knew she understood me. I kissed her forehead, then wheeled her in front of the television. It wouldn't be long before they would leave and I'd be on the nine-fifteen bus heading to my new home.

I stood outside of the orphanage, holding my belly in pain. I was experiencing sharp cramps after running here from the bus stop half a mile away. Once I caught my breath, I decided to walk up the steps to the porch and knock on the door.

An old elderly lady with short curly white hair, dressed like a nun, answered, displaying a confused look on her face.

"Hi, my name is Gracie Edmond, and I came because I need a place to live," I said, holding back tears.

"Gracie, do your parents know you're here?" she asked, looking down the road before welcoming me in.

Inside was spacious, filled with ancient furniture, dusty artwork and dreary curtains. The color scheme throughout was burgundy, black, and gold. The shades were drawn shut, and I didn't hear any of the young girls I imagined would be running around filling the house with laughter.

"No, they don't because that's who I'm trying to get away from. My family has been molesting me for years and I'm scared to go back home," I explained.

"Oh, you poor thing. Sit right here I'll be right back," she ordered, pointing to a cherry wood bench in the foyer.

It was now eleven in the afternoon, so I was sure Carl was home and noticed I was gone. Over the next few days, I would brainstorm ways to get my sister out. She wasn't able to speak for herself, so if I called the cops, they'd have no way of asking her what happened.

"Gracie, this is Sue-Ellen. She is the director of the orphanage and wants to know more about you," the nun stated, displaying a fake smile.

"Well, long story short, my father and brother have been raping me senseless, and my mother won't do anything to stop it because she's an alcoholic. I saw this number in the phone book and figured it would be a fresh start," I vented.

"And are you also with child?" Sue asked, looking at my belly.

"Yes, not sure how far along I am, but as you can see, I'm starting to show," I said, rubbing my stomach.

Sue whispered in the nun's ear, then looked at me and smiled.

"Come, dear, let me show you your new room. Im Sister Marsha, ill get you acclimated" the nun said, grabbing my hand.

We walked up the carpeted staircase and down a hall that had several doors lined up on each side, like a hotel. The house was an old Victorian style, huge with very outdated wallpaper and fixtures.

At the end of the hall was a door with the number two on it. The nun walked me in, took my travel bag, and gave me a long sleeve black dress to wear. Inside the room were two beds. On the one to the left, there was a young black girl who appeared to be sick. Not only was she sweating, but her lips were dry, ashy, and chattering.

"Helen, say hi to your new roommate, Gracie," the nun demanded.

The girl looked over at me with fear in her eyes. It reminded me of how I looked every time Carl came into my room at night.

"Dinner starts at five, Gracie, so be at the table on time. Helen, I'll bring up your share when I get a chance," she said before walking out.

I changed my clothes and sat next to Helen on her bed.

"Something doesn't seem right. Are you okay?" I inquired.

She looked around as if she was making sure the coast was clear before speaking. This girl literally looked petrified and traumatized, as if she saw a ghost.

"Helen, talk to me. No need to be scared we are safe now," I consoled.

She shook her head no, then pointed to her dresser and pulled the blanket up to her neck.

When I opened the top drawer, Polaroid pictures were sitting on top. As I went thru them, I could see she was pregnant once upon a time. Her belly was huge and what looked to be her family was gathered around, celebrating her baby shower. She looked like a totally different person. The girl in those photos was lively, vibrant, and smiling from ear to ear. I wondered when the baby was born because she was not only dangerously skinny, but very young.

"Helen, where is your baby?" I asked.

She shrugged her shoulders, and tears began to buildup in her eyes.

I hated seeing anyone cry, so I embraced her with a warm, tight hug.

"It's ok sweetie, I'm here with you now everything will be okay."

I went to release my grip, and she pulled me in closer as if this was the first hug she received in years.

"G-get o-out of here p-please, I b-beg you," she stuttered.

"Why?" I asked, confused.

Once again, she looked around and glanced at the door before answering.

"They took my baby and s-sold it t-to the black market. The priest from the church we attend on Sundays p-performed the delivery and w-wouldn't allow me to hold him after birth," she broke down.

I covered my mouth in shock. Get dressed we'll find another orphanage to go to," I insisted.

"O-once you w-walk in the door is locked b-behind you with a padlock that only the director and other nuns have a key to open. Me and y-you are the only two black g-girls here and our babies get sold right after birth. Infants aren't allowed h-here, but they never told me t-that," she whimpered, wiping snot off her face.

I ran to the window to see what the nearest business was, but only saw a Catholic church in sight. When I tried to open the window I met resistance, I examined closer and noticed it was bolted shut.

At that very moment, I reached for my purse to call the police, but it wasn't there. The nun had taken it when she walked out of the room.

"So if the doors and windows are locked, what's another way to escape?" I panicked, looking around.

"Nothing we can do, Gracie. The whole outside is wired with cameras and no girl is to leave the premises without the supervision of a nun," Helen informed me, finally sitting up straight in her bed.

I paced the room, contemplating if I should break the window and jump out.

"Won't work," Helen said, interrupting my strategy.

"What won't work?"

"The window. I saw you looking at it but the glass is shatter and soundproof. Plus, the jump is fifteen feet high so you wouldn't survive. I thought about the same thing a few months ago until my last roommate brought it to my attention," she explained.

"What happened to her?" I gulped.

"She tried to make a run for it after church one day, but once she got to the corner, she was attacked by the orphanage dog. He's a German Shepard named Saint who was trained by the priest to sniff out and chase anyone that tried to escape the property. Since the church is across the street, the supervising nun ran to the house and let him out of the basement. I was shocked when she was carried back to the room by Sue-Ellen. Unconscious, bloody, and missing a finger," Helen explained.

"Where is she now?" I asked, still in shock.

"She was sold to a white family in Alabama. They changed her name and use her to do sixteen hours of labor on the family farm each day. Ever since that incident, I never thought about escaping again," she whispered, looking around.

"What made her come to this orphanage in the first place?" I questioned.

"Her mother stabbed her one day because she wouldn't willingly sleep with a drug dealer for money. One night she vented to me and said she doesn't have any memory of when her mother was sober and not strung out on drugs. She had a bad crack addiction that cost eight hundred dollars a week. When the money went dry, the dealer said he'll take twelve-year-old pussy in exchange for a few rocks, so her own mother assisted him in tying her down and allowed her to be raped for two hours straight with no care in the world. The whole time she was in the bathroom getting high with the door locked, peeking through the shades. She said when he was on top she dug into the drug dealer's eyes so her mom grabbed a knife and stabbed her several times in the legs. The next day she managed to peel herself off the floor and took the train here but never called the police," Helen went on.

"What made her want to run from this orphanage, though. Was she pregnant?" I questioned further.

"Well, she ran from here because she had just learned it was her turn to get impregnated by the priest," Helen revealed.

My heart instantly sank into my stomach. I backed up against the wall and slid onto the floor.

"I just couldn't catch a break," I said to myself, finally releasing the tears I held in all day.

CHAPTER FOUR

AFTER SOBBING FOR THIRTY MINUTES, I realized I came too far to stop now. Images of Nettie enduring rape from both my brother and father made my spirit perk up and brainstorm more ideas. I sat on the hard twin mattress and observed my surroundings. The wallpaper was a dingy yellow and peeling in three different spots. Cobb webs swept across the corners of the ceiling, and the smell of mildew filled my nostrils. I looked at the clock and saw it was five minutes before dinner. I wiped my face and gave Helen another hug.

"We will make it out of here, I promise."

I looked into her brown watery eyes, then kissed her forehead.

"I'll be back," I said, walking out.

When I stepped out of the room, two little white girls jumped back, holding hands. The closeness, similar faces, and matching dresses were a dead giveaway. They were twins.

"See Maggie, this is where they keep the monkeys," the taller one laughed.

These girls couldn't be any older than seven, so I brushed off the ignorant comment and realized this was only taught behavior and they didn't know better.

"Hi, I'm Gracie what's y'all's name?" I asked, killing them with kindness.

They both looked at me in awe. I could tell that inside they were just as scared as I was, but were trying to cover it up with laughter. The taller one was more outspoken and courageous, while the shorter twin came off shy and innocent.

"Dinner is ready, girls!" a voice yelled from downstairs.

The twins skipped off, still hand in hand, never answering my question. I followed close behind them, making sure not to get lost in this huge Victorian house.

As I walked past the front door, I realized Helen wasn't kidding when she said the doors were padlocked. It was conveniently high enough that none of the girls here could reach it, and it didn't take long before I realized I was the oldest.

The smell of beef and baked bread entered my nose as I walked into the kitchen.

"Everyone say hello to Gracie. She is our new housemate, and I expect you all to treat her with respect," the nun from earlier announced.

About twelve little white faces all turned and gawked at me, including the twins. They ranged from six to about eleven years old and all wore grey knitted, knee-length dresses with black tights.

"That seat is for you," an elderly overweight white woman wearing an apron pointed with a spoon.

I sat next to a cute little girl with two braids who looked to be about eight. Her face was angelic, with a few speckled brown freckles on her cheeks.

The lady with the apron started serving food at the head of the table. What looked to be shepherd's pie was dropped into each bowl, causing a loud thud.

"What's your name?" I asked the little girl.

She whispered "Gabby". Her beautiful innocent soft voice made me wondered why she was here. She didn't look white, but she didn't look black so I knew she had to be mixed but I couldn't tell with what.

"Why are you here Gabby?" I pried.

"My mother dropped me off and never came back." Her voice cracked.

"No talking at the dinner table! Gabby, you know better," the cook shouted.

I wanted so badly to yell back and defend her, but I didn't want to become a target. When she walked away and I asked Gabby what that woman's name was. She looked around a few times before softly uttering, "Margie."

Once again, the twins were eyeing me as if they were going to tell. I also noticed all the other girls got a big piece of warm bread, except Gabby and me. In my peripherals, I watched Sister Marsha walk up the stairs carrying a plate with a peanut butter sandwich and a glass of water. I guess she was bringing Helen her rations.

After supper, I rushed back to my room. When I got to the top landing Sister Marsha was feeling on the hallway wall, crying. She jumped back at the sound of my foot touching a squeaky floorboard.

"Ah, Gracie, you startled me," she said, wiping a black tear off her face.

I was shocked to see she wore eyeliner and mascara, being a nun and all. The look she had was as if she was hiding something and couldn't hold it in any longer. I gazed into her ice-blue eyes and got the chills.

"Sorry sister Marsha. I was just going to my room," I replied.

When I walked past her, I noticed a white plastered patch where she was touching. Something was off about this lady, but I couldn't put my finger on it just yet.

I raced into my room without looking back and slammed the door behind me.

"You okay, Gracie?" Helen questioned, jumping up.

"I think Sister Marsha has some sick emotional attachment to this house. I could have sworn I just saw her caressing the wall while sobbing."

Helen made a face and looked down at her sandwich as if she didn't want to talk about it.

"What? Did I miss something?" I barked.

"If you haven't noticed, Sister Marsha isn't your typical nun. She is a sinner, and it eats her up every day knowing she is a hypocrite. One of the older girls here said she's been having an affair with the priest for decades. Sad to say, but they were happy when his wife died before ever finding out the truth about them. Since nuns aren't supposed to have sex, nobody ever knew this was going on until one day this girl, Sally, who went missing, saw her putting a dead infant into the wall. If you walk around the house, you'll notice three plastered spots throughout. That means she was pregnant a total of three times. When the director asked her about it, she said the walls were weakening so she had to do some patchwork in a few areas. Granted, this all happened twenty years ago, but you're not the first to catch her doing that," Helen whispered.

This place was really creepy, and the thought of them taking my child and selling it made me even sicker. I didn't know how I was going to sleep knowing there were dead babies in the wall.

CHAPTER FIVE

THE NEXT MORNING, I was awoken by Helen, who was standing over me yelling.

"Gracie, wake up! Our priest, Father Mark, will be here any minute to meet you," she said frantically.

"Wait, won't I meet him Sunday in church?" I asked, wiping crust out my eyes.

"He meets all new girls the first forty-eight hours after they arrive. Depending on his observation and assessment they may handle you differently seeing you're with child and all. Even though he isn't a trained doctor, the orphanage uses him as such. Real doctors are obligated to report anything they think is abuse so we will never see anyone that's credentialed in here. Since most girls are being molested or have injuries from abuse, they don't let outsiders in under any circumstances. Father Mark delivered my baby on an old dusty bed down in the basement. He even does small procedures on some of the girls, but I've heard horror stories," Helen went on.

"Like what?" I pried with big eyes.

"Well, this little white girl named Luna needed her tonsils out because they kept getting infected, so Father Mark gathered up his medical instruments and did the job. Every night while she was in recovery, he went into her room and forced her into oral sex. He said something about how she didn't have a gag reflex anymore, so it felt better. Luna hasn't been the same since. This happened when she was six and still at the age of eight she will not speak to anyone. She shakes her head or points but will not talk. Any sudden noises will cause her to jump in fear and hide," Helen explained.

"Wow, poor girl," I uttered with my head down.

"Knock knock."

We both turned to see a heavyset elderly man walk in. By the way he was dressed, it had to be Father Mark. He stepped in wearing a black blazer, white button-down, and a clerical collar. He was short, round, ugly, and grey-haired. I swallowed my spit and grimaced at the fact that this was the man impersonating a doctor in an all girl orphanage.

"Oh, you must be Gracie. You're beautiful for a black girl," he blurted out, extending his hand looking over thick-framed glasses.

I made a face and scrunched my eyebrows together at his comment.

"Hi," I mumbled, without eye contact.

"Nice to meet you. I heard you're expecting so before lunch today you and I will go into the basement and get an ultrasound. I also have all the equipment to deliver the baby when the time comes. Right now we just want to see how far along you are and what the gender is," he stated, eyeing my belly.

He reached out to rub my stomach, but I stepped back, stopping him in his tracks. He looked up, shocked that I resisted his gesture. His skin was pale, but the bags under his eyes were red. Father Mark looked like a gremlin who had pointy ears, two facial moles, a beer belly, and rotten teeth.

"Feisty one, huh?" he laughed, walking out the door with a wave and creepy smile.

CHAPTER SIX

AFTER BREAKFAST, Sister Marsha told me to follow her to the basement where Father Mark was waiting. As I walked down the dusty old stairs, I clutched my belly afraid of what he might do. Even though this was an incest baby, it was clear that I would have to carry to full term. If Suzette had gotten an abortion when she got pregnant with my brother's kid, Nettie wouldn't be here. I thanked God for that girl every day because she motivated me, even more, to leave that place and seek help. I felt bad leaving her but I couldn't risk getting locked in that room for four more days again.

"Ahhh, Gracie, nice to see you again," Father Mark grinned, looking like a devil wearing latex gloves.

Next to him was a portable ultrasound machine, a leather recliner with holes, and a tray covered with a sheet.

Sister Marsha walked upstairs and locked the door behind her.

"Come now, Gracie, let's see what gender you have in there," he said, tapping the recliner.

Eager to get this done and over with, I walked over and laid down. The basement gave me haunted vibes and was very cold. I inhaled deeply, shut my eyes, and pulled up my black dress.

"Those, too," he blurted out, pointing at my panties.

"Why? I thought this was just a stomach ultrasound!" I yelled, jumping up.

He pulled the sheet off the tray, revealing a vaginal speculum and lube.

"No, my precious darling. I need to take a look at your cervix to make sure everything is progressing normally," he said with that stupid grin again.

"No!" I screamed, kicking the tray over.

"Sister!" He growled, clenching his fist.

Sister Marsha swung open the door and ran down, ready to answer his command.

"Bring the leather restraints," he ordered.

Sister Marsha rushed over with a bucket and they both tried pinning me to the chair as I kicked and screamed. Father Mark punched me in the face a few times in an attempt to get me to stop flailing.

There was no way I was letting him open up my vagina.

"Grab her feet, Marsha. I got her hands," Father Mark yelled as he tightened the straps to the recliner.

I spit in his accomplices face so she elbowed me in the chin, causing me to see stars and halos. Before I knew it, I was in four-point restraints, unable to move with my legs spread apart. Father Mark put on his gloves and poured lube onto the speculum.

He put it inside me and cranked it all the way open, trying to make me pay for not cooperating.

"Ahh, it's nice and pink, just how it's supposed to be, my dear. No sign of an infection and only thing in there is your cervix," he smiled.

"Do you feel pain when I do this?" He asked, circling his fingers around the wall of my vagina.

"No," I cringed.

"How bout there?"

"No."

He smiled as he admired the glossy speculum he just took out.

"Alright time to see what we're having," he said, pouring lube on my belly.

Father Mark glided the probe across my stomach until we heard a heartbeat. I let out a sigh of relief, shocked that all this stress didn't cause a miscarriage.

"I see it," Sister Marsha blurted out with excitement.

"It's a boy!" Father Mark announced.

They both jumped for joy as if it were their baby.

Due to all the pain in my swollen face, I couldn't smile, but I was happy. I wanted so badly to get him tested for any defects, but I knew they wouldn't take me to the hospital. Maybe if he was a handicapped baby, they'd let me keep him. I was sure those infants were harder to sell.

"Alright go upstairs with Marsha and get washed up," Father Mark demanded as he untied me.

I did as I was told and followed her upstairs.

"Go in there and wait while I get you a change of clothes." She pointed to the bathroom.

I walked in, sat on the floor, and pondered once again on a way out of here.

CHAPTER SEVEN

After I washed up I went to my room to talk to Helen but she wasn't there. I was sure she was wondering why I didn't come up after breakfast. I looked out the window and saw all the girls running in the recess yard. Before walking out, I looked in the mirror and noticed the whole right side of my face was bruised. I couldn't believe I left a house of abuse to come here and endure the same thing.

When I walked down the hall, I noticed Sister Marsha rubbing the wall again, as if she was reminiscing about the past. She was very creepy and only did that when she thought nobody was around. I tiptoed past her and made my way out the back door. The whole yard was enclosed by a metal gate that had barbed wire along the top. All the girls here had to be brainwashed if they were able to look past everything going on and just play. Every day, we got two hours outside so the housekeepers could clean and lunch could be prepared. I glanced around, looking for Helen, and spotted her a few feet away, glaring through the fence.

"Hey, Helen, everything okay?" I asked, looking at her face.

She seemed panicked and anxious, like the day I met her.

"No, Gracie, I have to get out of here. I overheard the director saying she found a family for me in Virginia. They offered five thousand dollars, and Father Mark accepted. I'm going to be a locked away house slave!" she cried, gripping the fence.

"Shh, don't worry. I'll get you out of here before that happens," I reassured her.

"You can't! Don't you see this is all pointless? I don't know how much more I can take," Helen cried.

"Let's sneak to the side of the house and see if the basement door is unlocked. I noticed a set of keys on a hook during my ultrasound," I suggested.

Helen wiped her face and followed a good distance behind me so nobody would suspect we were up to anything together. Hopefully, the key would unlock the front door and we could make a run for it. I looked around the yard one more time before reaching for the doorknob.

"It's unlocked," I whispered, grabbing her hand.

We both tiptoed across the cement floor in total darkness.

"I never been down here before it's scary," Helen gulped.

"There's the key let's try it!" I shouted as I snatched it off the hook. We rushed over to the stairs but were stopped in our tracks by a little white girl. She stood in front of us and said nothing like she was hypnotized or in a trance. Her eyes were big and blue and if I had to guess she was about six years old.

"Hi, I'm Gracie and this is Helen. We were just coming down to look for something are you lost?" I asked.

She gazed into my eyes with a cold, blank stare and didn't say a word.

"Do you want me to bring you to the recess yard?" I offered.

Still nothing, so I decided to walk past her and continue our mission.

"Sister! Sister! they're trying to escape!" she yelled when she noticed the keys in my hand.

Suddenly the dog started barking from behind a closed door, scaring Helen and me to death.

I dropped the keys and ran back to the side door, scared Sister Marsha would see us and release the Shepard.

"Go hurry," Helen said, running behind me.

When we made it outside, we both clutched our chests, trying to catch our breath.

"I think they hypnotized her because she was normal the other day. Maybe they put her down there to guard the keys and make sure nobody escapes," I said, returning to the yard.

"See, we are trapped," Helen huffed, slapping her thigh.

"There has to be a way out of here. Let's go in the house, sneak to the front room and climb out a window," I suggested.

"The kitchen is right there. I'm sure Sister Marsha or the cook, Margie, will see us," Helen mentioned.

"We have to exhaust all options. It's better than sitting here."

I grabbed her hand and crept to the back door. Scanning the house, nobody was in sight, but the director's office was next to the entrance. I noticed a door that looked like a closet in the dining room so I ran over to it thinking we should hide in there until the coast was clear. The minute I opened the door, a young girl's cry pierced my ears.

"Help me, please!" she cried.

On the bed in front of us was a little girl pinned down in four-point restraints. She looked pale, malnourished, frightened, and helpless.

Without thinking, Helen and I ran over and unbuckled the thick brown leather straps. Her wrist had dried blood and scraps on them from fighting to get loose.

The poor thing was sweaty, fragile, and so pale she almost looked translucent.

"He r-raped me," she stuttered through dusty blue lips.

Helen and I stood on opposite sides of her so she could use our bodies as a crutch. She limped in pain as we scurried across the wooden floor, trying not to make it squeak. When I looked both ways, there was still nobody in sight. As much as we wanted to escape this place, we couldn't leave her there to get raped again. I'd never want someone to endure the same experience I did.

"Thanks for saving me," she sniffled as we made it outside.

"Don't tell anyone about this, or Helen and I will get in trouble. It's almost time for dinner, so make sure to stop upstairs and change out of those torn clothes. We are going to walk to the other side of the yard so they don't think we're up to something," I said, grabbing Helen's hand and walking off as if she was Nettie.

CHAPTER EIGHT

"Dinner!" Sister Marsha yelled across the recess yard.

All the girls formed into a single file line as if they were in the military.

I watched as the twins held hands and sat next to each other at the table. They went everywhere together and I couldn't help but wonder how they too ended up here. Gabby sat next to me as the other girls raced to pick a seat.

"Helen, your dinner will be brought to you later. Make your way to the study," Sue-Ellen ordered, walking in unexpectedly.

I was shocked she didn't hear us let the little girl out earlier because her office was only a few feet away. She spent a lot of time in there and only showed her face when necessary.

Helen released my hand and followed the instructions. The study was down the hall and we weren't allowed in unless authorized.

Margie, the orphanage cook, came out with a big silver saucepan and a matching ladle. She began serving chicken noodle soup with a slice of bread, one by one.

"I have to use the bathroom," I lied as I saw Sister Marsha and Sue-Ellen walking into her office and shutting the door. I pressed my ear against the cold wood to hear what they were saying.

"The family that wants Helen called saying they just found out their daughter can no longer bear children. Long story short, they asked if I could insert the husband's sperm inside Helen. They still want her sent over to be their servant, but want to add a baby into the contract. This could bring in some good money, Marsha," Sue confessed.

"How do you plan on orchestrating that?" Sister Marsha replied.

"She sent me the semen already. All I need now is the sedatives, turkey baster, and leather restraints."

My heart sank as I ran to the study to warn Helen. She was sitting on the carpet, rocking back and forth, wiping away her tears. This was the day she had been dreading for months.

"They want you to be the surrogate for the daughter of the family you're going to," I blurted out.

"Are you serious? This can't be true," Helen whimpered.

I snatched a handful of tissue out of the box sitting on the desk and passed it to her.

"I can't take it anymore!" she cried, slapping the floor with fury.

"Don't worry. Tonight I'm going to explore every inch of this house to find a way out of here for us. I won't let them take you," I reassured her.

Helen blew her nose a few times before answering, then finally looked up at me and said, "I hope so, Gracie. I hope so."

———

After dinner, I went to my room and noticed Helen was still in the study. It had been two hours since they took her, so I wondered what was taking so long.

While the rest of the girls were getting ready for bed, I decided to start packing what little I had. They took my belongings when I got here, so I tossed mine and Helen's undergarments into a small waste basket trash bag. Tonight I had to find a way out of this demented house so that Helen wouldn't be sold.

I sat on the edge of the bed and wondered what Nettie was doing right now. I missed her but at the same time was happy she didn't come. The nuns and priests were psychopaths and would have sold her to a white man to serve as a raping post.

The darker the sky got, the more doubtful I became about finding an escape route.

"Now eat your sandwich and get some rest," Sister Marsha snapped as she pushed Helen into the room.

Helen was holding a peanut butter sandwich and a glass of water. Her hands were shaking, almost causing her to drop her dinner. She walked in like a baby deer fresh out of the womb; frightened with wobbly legs. The sedatives hadn't worn off, causing her to be drowsy.

"Oh, my God, are you okay?" I asked once the door shut.

"No! I fought and kicked, but it was no use. They shoved a turkey baster inside of me that was filled with semen and that was all I remember."

Helen didn't have any underwear on and was now wearing a ripped, oversized white t-shirt and socks.

Residual semen was sliding down her thigh, causing me to gag.

"It's nine now, so the nuns should be in bed very soon. I was going to look around for open windows, doors, spare keys, and a weapon," I informed Helen, trying to change the topic.

"Gracie, just stop! Don't you think other girls have done what you're trying to do already? We're doomed, don't you get it? Stop with the optimist hero bull crap and become a realist. Just like you couldn't do anything earlier you to save me, you can't do anything now," she yelled releasing built-up frustrations.

I couldn't blame her for not having hope. She had been here for nearly a year, and it had only gotten worse. The only thing keeping me going was my baby and Nettie.

"I'm not giving up on us," I reassured her once more.

She took a towel and placed it between her legs to stop the constant flow. I could tell she was completely grossed out, ashamed, and fed up. It was a feeling I knew all too well.

"I packed our stuff so be awake just in case I find a way out of here tonight," I said before leaving the room.

The halls were quiet, and it appeared as though everyone was in bed. I tiptoed down the carpeted steps and went straight for the front door. It was secured by a chain, a latch and two padlocks. Next, I walked into the living room and tried all four windows, but they were all bolted shut. My next thought was the back door since we used it more often. That too was sealed tight with a chain and security code system. I ran to the study to see if there were any windows in there, but that door had also been secured shut. I decided not to enter the basement because the last thing I needed was for the dog to bark and wake up the whole house. Before going back upstairs, I rummaged through the kitchen drawer. There were no knives but a Philips screwdriver was sitting there looking just as good, so I snatched it up. Unfortunately, it became evident that the only way to escape was by murdering Marsha and Sue- Ellen. At that point, desperate times were calling for desperate measures. I put the screwdriver in my panties and tiptoed back to the stairs. As I put my foot on the bottom step, I was suddenly grabbed by the back of the neck and pulled down to the floor.

"So, you like being sneaky, huh?" I heard the priest say.

He snatched me by my ankles and dragged me down the basement stairs on my back. I protected the back of my head with my hands to stop it from hitting the hardwood on each step.

"Get off me!" I screamed, trying to release his hold.

When we reached the bottom, he swung me onto the side of the basement where the floor was covered with the type of blue mats you'd find in a school gym.

"You're supposed to be in bed, not creeping around this house. You won't be the first or the last looking for a way to escape. Tonight I'm going to teach you a lesson that's going to make you wish you never walked through those doors. I don't know why you colored girls think you could come in here trying to brainwash the rest of the children we have worked so hard to train," he muttered as he shuffled through drawers.

I tried to stand up and run, but I couldn't because my back was now in excruciating pain. My legs were ignoring the signals my brain was sending to run away.

"Ahh, perfect," he said, turning around, holding a plunger and rope.

Tears were now coming down my face, and saliva was seeping from the corners of my mouth. Even though I was five months pregnant, he forced me onto my stomach and pinned me down with his knee so he could tie my hands and feet together. Once my wrists were secured, he did the same to my ankles, then rolled me onto my back.

"Stop, you disgusting pig!" I yelled, hoping Helen would hear.

The priest was now hunched over me with a big smile, revealing every rotten tooth in his filthy mouth.

"Arf, arf, arf" the dog barked from behind the door.

Father Mark began sliding my panties down, surprised to see a screwdriver sitting on top of my vagina.

"Oh, little Miss Gracie is getting brave, huh? Not only were you creeping but you're stashing weapons," he said, picking it up and setting it to the side.

"You'll never get away with this! You're going to spend your life in prison when the authorities find out what you're doing to innocent girls," I cried.

"I've been doing this for over a decade, and as you can see, the orphanage is still up and running," he snapped, picking up the plunger.

"Wait! No! What are you doing?" I squirmed as he separated my pussy lips.

Before I knew it, he was shoving the wooden stick end of the plunger into my vagina.

"Ahhhhhhhhh fuck!" I screamed as the dry wood caused friction against my pussy walls.

I squeezed my eyes shut so I couldn't see the pleasure on his face as he mutilated me.

He did a few fast strokes that left blood on the stick.

Suddenly I felt his overgrown five o'clock shadow on my stomach.

He was rubbing his face on my belly with a smile only his mother would love.

"Ah, the baby is almost done cooking. The only reason I'm going to stop is so we don't cause contractions and make baby Isaac coming early." He gasped, looking at the plunger.

How dare he name my baby as if I was going to willingly hand him over? I was not going down without a fight, so they better be ready.

Father Mark took a pocketknife out and cut me loose.

"I better not see or hear about you trying to escape again, Gracie. Ask Helen how that worked out for the last girl that tried it," he said, confiscating the screwdriver and making his way up the stairs.

CHAPTER NINE

THE NEXT MORNING I woke up in bed with an oxygen mask on my face. The last thing I remembered was father Mark shoving a plunger up my vagina after he found me creeping around the orphanage. I tried to lift my arm to remove the mask, but my brain wouldn't send the message to my extremities. My whole body ached, and my head was pounding harder than my heart.

I looked around the room and noticed Helen wasn't in her bed. The clock showed it was recess time and almost time for dinner.

"Gracie, how are you feeling?"

Sue- Ellen, the director, asked as she stood in the doorway holding a pad and paper, looking very concerned.

"I was fine until Father Mark dragged me down a flight of wooden steps and badgered me with a plunger!" I barked.

"Well, to be fair, you weren't supposed to be out of your room. I'll talk to Father about being less aggressive with our pregnant girls from now on. As for you, please don't get caught wandering again because I can't promise that the consequences next time won't cost you your baby," she stated as she jotted down notes.

"How can you sleep at night as a woman knowing you're brainwashing and torturing young girls for a living?" I cried.

"Because I was born into this life and don't know any different. I was raised in this house and abandoned at a very young age. Forty-two years ago my parents knocked on that front door, handed me to my grandmother, and said they were going to the Navy. I was given a kiss on the cheek and told I'd be picked up in thirty days. I've been here ever since and never received one visit call or card. Granny died when I was nineteen and left this big ol' house to me. The void never goes away, Gracie. You just get stronger as the days go by," she confided before walking away.

I couldn't help but wonder what she meant by that, but it became obvious she had endured some serious trauma. Sue-Ellen was sicker than I thought, and I had to let Helen know right away.

When I lifted my head, I became dizzy and began seeing colorful spots. I mustered up enough strength to touch my forehead and noticed it was bandaged on the left side. Father Mark had caused more injuries than I thought. I just hoped none would affect the baby. Too weak to think any further, I dozed off, no longer able to fight the effects of the medications.

CHAPTER TEN

"Gracie."

I woke up suddenly to Helen's shaky voice. She was kneeling in front of me with tears streaming down her face.

"Look what they did to you! I'm next. I know it!" Helen cried, removing the oxygen mask.

"Father Mark sexually assaulted me two nights ago and I think I'm vaginally bleeding," I finally managed to say.

Helen lifted the bottom of my dress and confirmed that blood was oozing onto the thin, dingy white bed sheet. I wasn't sure who picked me up off the basement floor or what sedatives they gave me, but I was in a lot of pain. The bruises, welts, and blood were an indication he used excessive force with no regard to the life growing inside me.

I observed Helen and watched as she mentally connected the dots to everything that was happening. It was like she had frozen mid-conversation and had a flashback.

"It's all coming back now. They did the same thing to me when I was pregnant. I remember waking up on oxygen and dizzy from the amount of blood I had lost. The only difference is I woke up baby-less with Father Mark standing over my bed, showing rotten teeth. I was drugged and given a C-section under sedation. Never even got to meet my little man." Helen wept uncontrollably.

I grabbed my stomach, making sure it was still round and hard. It was. I caressed underneath my belly and searched for a scar. Nothing.

They wanted so badly to get their hands on my baby boy but I was too early in the pregnancy, unlike Helen, who was thirty-eight weeks when that happened.

The next morning when I woke up, I felt so discombobulated. The meds were finally wearing off, and I could feel the pain in my back increasing. The clock showed it was 5 in the morning, so breakfast was in two hours. I rubbed my crusted eyes and looked over to check on Helen, but she wasn't there. Normally she was scared to wander around the house alone, so I wondered where she could be. Tomorrow she was supposed to get picked up by her new white family, so I had to find a way out of here ASAP.

I looked out the foggy window and scanned the enclosed yard once again. The only other option I could think of was finding Helen now and hiding in the basement until they took the dog out for his morning walk. That would give us twenty minutes to fiddle with the locks without being heard. The kitchen was empty right now, so I was sure I could find a tool to tamper with the padlock.

I stuffed a few pairs of our underwear into a knapsack and tip-toed down the carpeted steps. My baby was moving and a sharp pain was radiating down my leg. Thoughts of seeing Nettie and taking her with me to a shelter were motivation to keep going.

The orphanage was quiet, and the sunlight was shining through the glass windows. Freedom was so close, but yet so far away. I searched the hallways, bathrooms, and living room, but still no sign of Helen. Maybe she had the same idea I did and was already in the basement, waiting. I crept to the kitchen to see what I could find in the drawers.

When I entered, I dropped to my knees at the sight of Helen hanging from the ceiling fan. Her fingertips, ears, and lips were bluish purple, indicating she had been here a while. The beautiful, thick afro she once wore was now stringy, oily, and stiff. I clutched my belly and sobbed on the tile floor, no longer caring about how loud I was. If only she could have just held it together one more day. I felt guilty for not acting fast enough and being too weak to wake up yesterday. I wiped the snot off my face and gained my composure. Before I headed to my room, I opened the kitchen drawer and snatched a butcher knife that wasn't there before. I knew one day they would be caught slipping, and this was exactly what I needed to help with my escape. At that point, I was fed up and ready to slice anyone that stood in my way. I was leaving this place whether they liked it or not. The next person that obstructed my path was getting butterflied like a piece of shrimp.

Just as I was about to head up the stairs, I heard Sue-Ellen whispering in her office. I walked up closer and concentrated to hear what she was saying through the thick old wooden doors.

"I apologize, Mr. O'Neil but we can't control these things. This is the third girl to hang herself in the past six years and we are doing our best to get a handle on things," she assured.

The room got quiet for three minutes so I assumed the man on the other end was saying his piece.

"I understand completely. I'm sorry your daughter is dealing with these infertility issues it must be frustrating. That leads me to the next option we have. There is a fourteen-year-old girl here named Gracie, who is already pregnant. Now I know you wanted to use your son-in-law's sperm, but this is an alternative to speed up the process. She is expecting an African American baby boy in about four months," Sue-Ellen informed.

I covered my mouth and began to tremble.

"Perfect! I'm glad you're willing to accept her, Mr. O'Neil. I'll type up a new contract shortly and have her ready by noon tomorrow. In the meantime, let me go cut this imbecile off the ceiling fan before the rest of the girls wake up."

I gasped and lightly ran up the stairs to my room. If I couldn't get out by tonight, I'd end up doing the same thing Helen did. At least my baby would be in heaven with me.

CHAPTER ELEVEN

I PACED my room with the knife in my hand, plotting the next move. Sue-Ellen was currently cleaning up the suicide, so there was no way to sneak past her right now. Suddenly the door flew open and Father Mark walked in. I hid the weapon behind my back and acted as normally as possible.

"Well, hello, Gracie, how are you feeling? Do you need more pain meds for your back?" he asked.

"Uh, yeah, that would be great," I replied, sticking my hand out.

"Here you go, my dear," he said, preparing to drop pills in my hand.

As he walked closer to me, I pulled the knife out and stabbed him repeatedly in the stomach. The pills fell to the floor, and after a few more jabs, so did he. I searched his pockets and found a ring of keys and twenty bucks. Tears fell from my eyes onto his big belly as I looked for a cell phone. My heart was hurting because I really wished Helen held on one more day. I wiped my nose and stood up while holding my lower back. No phone, but that was the least of my worries.

When I heard Sue-Ellen return to her office, I crept back downstairs and waited on the bottom step to make sure the coast was clear.

All the lights were still off, but Helen's body was now cut free and hidden. I slowly walked to the front door and tried all three keys on the ring. Since Father Mark had just arrived, the alarm system was off. That had to be God because that door was never left unsecured. The gold key unlocked the bottom, and the silver unlatched the top. The loud metal click made my heart sink, and I could have sworn Sue-Ellen would hear me. When I heard her continue a phone conversation, I opened the door, allowing a ray of sunlight to shine in. I squinted my eyes and felt the blood flow to my feet, preparing me to run.

Before I knew it, I was clutching my belly, running down a dirt road to the bus stop with no shoes. Twenty dollars was enough to get me back home to

Nettie and make a couple of calls on a payphone if I had to. My hair was in a matted ponytail and my smooth dark skin was now scarred, ashy, and covered with bruises.

"Are you okay?" a woman asked as I crossed a busy intersection.

Her eyes went from my belly to the bandage on my forehead, then to my feet. I so badly wanted to tell her what was going on, but then I would have to tell her I killed the priest.

"I'm fine," I sputtered, running to the bus that pulled up a few feet away.

Two black women and a white man were rolling dice at the bus stop but didn't pay me any mind as I sped past them.

I knew that as soon as I got to the house I would have to open the white pages and look for a nearby shelter right away because I knew my father would put me six feet under for the stunt I pulled. After what I endured to keep my son alive, there was no way I could give him up for adoption now. The fact that he was still growing and moving proved God never took his hands off me.

I tapped the buzzer on the bus so the driver could let me off. My house was at the corner and I needed time to think of what to tell my family. The chance of Carl beating and raping me was high because I was supposed to be his sex toy, not Nettie. I brushed my hands down my dress, trying to remove the lint and wrinkles. The last thing I wanted was to walk in, looking defeated and weak. Saving Nettie was my only reason for ever returning to this house. I made her a promise, and I was the only person she could trust in this world, so I had to keep it.

I walked up the porch steps to my old residence and began to have flashbacks and PTSD. All the pain, trauma, and abuse came rushing back like it happened yesterday. Carl's car wasn't in the driveway, which was a good sign for me. I rang the bell and took a step back, scared at the face that would appear. When I heard footsteps, I cradled my belly and prepared for the worst.

"Hi, can I help you?" a white woman in her thirties with blonde hair asked, confused.

I looked at the number on the house, then looked past her to see the inside. The décor was different and the walls had been painted.

"I lived here with my family three weeks ago. Where did they go?"

"Oh, sweetie, I'm sorry, but my husband and I brought this house two weeks ago and hired an agent to handle the process. I wish I could tell you more, but all I know was that the sellers were in a rush to get out of town. Do you need help finding them?" she inquired, very concerned. Her eyes were resting on the blood splatter across my thighs from stabbing father Mark.

I covered my mouth and sat on the top stair in disbelief. They took Nettie and moved away out of fear of me telling the cops on them.

"Can I see your white pages?" I asked, wiping away a stream of tears.

"Sure," she replied, entering the house.

She came back with the book and a glass of lemonade.

I flipped through it and looked for the battered woman and children's shelter. When the white woman walked back into the house, I tore out the page I needed and stuffed it into my bra. My instinct was telling me she went inside to call the police. I guzzled down the drink, then took off running.

Made in the USA
Middletown, DE
06 September 2022